MW00876750

For Charlotte Rose Hearne

G. P. PUTNAM'S SONS
an imprint of Penguin Random House LLC
375 Hudson Street
New York, NY 10014

Copyright © 2016 by Jan Brett.
Penguin supports copyright. Copyright fuels creativity, encourages diverse voices, promotes free speech,
and creates a vibrant culture. Thank you for buying an authorized edition of this book and for complying with
copyright laws by not reproducing, scanning, or distributing any part of it in any form without permission.
You are supporting writers and allowing Penguin to continue to publish books for every reader.

G. P. Putnam's Sons is a registered trademark of Penguin Random House LLC.

Library of Congress Cataloging-in-Publication Data is available upon request.

Manufactured in China by RR Donnelley Asia Printing Solutions Ltd.
ISBN 978-0-399-17071-3
1 3 5 7 9 10 8 6 4 2

Design by Marikka Tamura.
Text set in LTC Cloister.
The art for this book was done in watercolors and gouache.
Airbrush backgrounds by Joseph Hearne.

"Everyone in the village is talking about the Christmas Festival," Matti told the Gingerbread Baby.

"I can sing in my Gingerbread Band!" the Gingerbread Baby sang out.

Matti laughed. "But you don't have a band."

Then Matti had an idea. "Gingerbread Baby, practice your best song.
I think I can help." And he hurried off to fetch the old cookbook.

In no time, Matti had mixed the ingredients, rolled out the dough and popped the gingerbread into the oven.

Bake a full eight minutes, the cookbook read. *DO NOT* peek.
Tick, tock, tick. Six minutes went by. Matti peeked.
Out of the oven came musical instruments, all made of gingerbread.

They danced onto the table, playing as they went. The instruments clamored to perform then and there, but Matti toned them down.

"First, you need some frosting," Matti said.
"Then we'll be off to the village."

The Gingerbread Baby was first in line, practicing his singing as he went. "Do, re, mi!"

Then came the Gingerbread Band. A violin, cello, double bass, French horn, clarinet and trumpet, tooting and zumming to the beat of the big bass drum.

They bounced along, playing
a march, with the Gingerbread Baby
leading the way.

Down in the village, the Gingerbread Baby and all the gingerbread instruments strutted onstage and began to play.

The villagers appeared from up the street, down the street,
and out their doors. Wild animals peered through the trees.

"Look at those instruments playing a tune!" a boy sang out.
"And a snappy one at that," a girl said, tapping her foot.

The Gingerbread Band played so sweetly
that everyone just had to dance.

The Gingerbread Baby saw the animals inch closer.
Aha, he thought, *I have just the music for them.* And he struck up
"The Wild Animals' Waltz."

The instruments played faster and faster.
No one was left standing still.

In the middle of the festivities, little Ann-Sophie stepped in closer.
"I think those instruments are really cookies," she announced.
"And I *so* want one!"

Everyone stared at the stage, thinking, *I want a piece of gingerbread
for myself.*

To distract them, the Gingerbread Baby began
singing a beautiful song.

"Stars twinkle, twinkle in the night,
Silver trees and snow delight,
Hand in hand, we twirl around,
Twirling to the magic sound."

The villagers were spellbound. Nobody noticed
the instruments behind him, quietly leaving the stage.

Backstage, Matti knew that the jig was up. He made a plan
to hide the Gingerbread Band.

While the Gingerbread Baby was singing, he scooped up
the snow and did a little magic where no one could see.

When the Gingerbread Baby saw that the gingerbread instruments were safe, he changed his tune.

"I am the Gingerbread Baby,
Just try to catch me!
Look all around,
But you'll never guess where I'll be!"

And he did a backflip off the stage, where Matti was waiting.

The Gingerbread Baby zigged and zagged.
"Catch him!" a boy yelled.

"We want that rascally baby," a girl called out.
He was headed toward the big Christmas tree when he disappeared.

The villagers looked and looked, but the Gingerbread Baby
had vanished into thin air, and the gingerbread instruments
were nowhere to be seen.